For Silas and Lila, whose ridiculous impressions
of tiny T. rex arms inspired it —A.L.

For Sprocket & Nova, ever my furry muses —S.L.

Text copyright © 2021 by Anna Lazowski
Jacket art and interior illustrations copyright © 2021 by Stephanie Laberis

All rights reserved. Published in the United States by Doubleday, an imprint of
Random House Children's Books, a division of Penguin Random House LLC, New York.

Doubleday and the colophon are registered trademarks of
Penguin Random House LLC.

Visit us on the Web! rhcbooks.com

Educators and librarians, for a variety of teaching tools, visit us at
RHTeachersLibrarians.com

Library of Congress Cataloging-in-Publication Data
Names: Lazowski, Anna, author. | Laberis, Steph, illustrator.
Title: T. rexes can't tie their shoes / by Anna Lazowski ; illustrated by Steph Laberis.
Description: New York : Doubleday, an imprint of Random House Children's Books,
[2021] | Audience: Ages 3–5. | Summary: "A humorous, alphabetical look at all the
things animals can't do but kids can" —Provided by publisher.
Identifiers: LCCN 2020011484 (print) | LCCN 2020011485 (ebook)
ISBN 978-0-593-18138-6 (hardcover) | ISBN 978-0-593-18139-3 (library binding) |
ISBN 978-0-593-18140-9 (ebook)
Subjects: LCSH: Animals—Miscellanea—Juvenile fiction. | Alphabet books. |
Picture books for children. | CYAC: Animals—Fiction. | Ability—Fiction. | Alphabet. |
Humorous stories. | LCGFT: Picture books. | Humorous fiction.
Classification: LCC PZ7.1.L387 Taam 2021 (print) | LCC PZ7.1.L387 (ebook) |
DDC 590 [E]—dc23

MANUFACTURED IN CHINA
10 9 8 7 6 5 4 3 2 1
First Edition

T. REXES CAN'T TIE THEIR SHOES

By **Anna Lazowski**

Illustrated by **Steph Laberis**

Doubleday Books for Young Readers

If you're still a bit small,
it is no fun at all
when you can't reach a shelf
or get dressed by yourself.

But you're not alone!
My dear friend, it is true:
Some things are *hard*—for animals too!
A hopscotching horse or kung fu kangaroo?

There are lots of things animals just cannot do. . . .

Alligators can't pick **a**pples.

Bees can't ride bicycles.

Cheetahs can't **c**hew bubble gum.

Dogs can't wash dishes.

Elephants can't fit in **e**levators.

Foxes can't **f**lip pancakes.

Giraffes can't do **g**ymnastics.

Horses can't play **h**opscotch.

Iguanas can't eat ice cream.

Jaguars can't do jumping jacks.

Kangaroos can't practice kung fu.

Llamas can't play leapfrog.

Monkeys can't do **m**agic tricks.

Narwhals can't eat nachos.

Owls can't fold **o**rigami.

Penguins can't **p**lay ping-**p**ong.

Quetzals can't keep **q**uiet.

Raccoons can't **ride** roller coasters.

Seahorses can't **s**ing.

T. rexes can't **t**ie their shoes.

Urchins can't open **u**mbrellas.

Vampire bats can't **v**acuum.

Walruses can't make **w**affles.

Xenopses can't play **x**ylophones.

Yaks can't throw **yo-yos.**

Zebras can't go **z**ip-lining.

But they can have a lot of fun trying!

Alligators can grow new teeth!
As alligators wear out or lose their teeth, new ones come in to replace them.

Bees can dance!
Bees use a waggle dance to tell other bees where to find food.

Cheetahs can run really fast!
In only three seconds, cheetahs can reach speeds of 70 miles (113 kilometers) per hour.

Dogs can see in the dark!
A dog's eye structure helps it see better in the dark than humans can. Dogs can also tell what's around them by using their whiskers, which are sensitive to air currents.

Elephants can make their own sunscreen!
Elephants use their trunks to cover their skin with sand and mud, to avoid sunburns.

Foxes are good listeners!
A fox can hear the slightest sound from many yards away. And it can rotate its ears to focus on different directions.

Giraffes can sleep standing up!
In the wild, giraffes usually sleep standing up so they're less vulnerable to predators.

Horses can walk as newborn babies!
A baby horse, called a foal, will usually stand up within an hour of being born.

Iguanas can grow a new tail!
If an iguana's tail is grabbed or injured, it can release the tail and grow a new one.

Jaguars can swim!
Unlike most cats, jaguars like the water. They can spread out their paws like flippers and hold their breath long enough to eat a meal underwater.

Kangaroos can jump really far!
A kangaroo can cover twenty-five feet (eight meters) in a single leap, thanks to its large feet and the springy tendons in its legs.

Llamas can carry a lot of stuff!
Llamas can weigh 440 pounds (200 kilograms) and can carry up to 25 percent of their weight. But if you put too much on them, they'll lie down and refuse to move.

Monkeys can balance!
Unlike humans and apes, most monkeys have tails, which help them climb trees and balance up high. They can even use their tails to pick things up!

Narwhals can change color!
Newborn narwhals start out a blue-gray shade, which darkens to bluish black when they're a little older. Adults are spotted gray and turn white as they grow old.

Owls can turn their heads almost all the way around!

Owls can turn their heads 270 degrees, which is like turning your head to the right until you're looking past your left shoulder.

Penguins can camouflage themselves!

The black back of a penguin blends into the dark ocean when seen from above. And predators swimming underneath have a hard time seeing a penguin's white belly against the bright surface of the water.

Quetzals can grow fancy feathers!

Male quetzals grow brightly colored tail feathers that form a three-foot (one-meter) train when they're trying to attract a female mate.

Raccoons can solve puzzles!

Raccoons are very smart and have extremely sensitive hands. They can use them to unlatch locks, open doors, and get into closed garbage cans to look for food.

Seahorses can help build robots!

Seahorses use their long tails to grab on to things. Robotics engineers have studied them to improve their ideas for building mechanical parts.

T. rexes could chomp!

T. rex had the strongest bite of any land animal that has ever lived, and it had the longest teeth of any dinosaur. Its arms were too short to put food in its mouth, so it used its huge jaws to crunch its prey.

Urchins can live for a long time!

Red sea urchins live in the shallow waters of the Pacific Ocean and can survive for more than two hundred years.

Vampire bats can sleep upside down!

Vampire bats sleep upside down, hanging from the roofs of caves. It keeps them out of harm's way and allows them to quickly swoop if danger approaches.

Walruses can live in the cold!

Walruses have their own insulation, a layer of blubber that keeps them warm in the icy-cold ocean.

Xenopses can hammer!

The xenops has an upturned beak that it uses to hammer into decaying wood, to look for insects.

Yaks can live very high up!

The lung capacity of a yak is three times that of a cow. This allows it to breathe the thin air high in the mountains of central Asia.

Zebras can be scanned like a bar code!

Every zebra has a stripe pattern that is unique. Scientists can use software to scan the stripes and identify each zebra in a herd.